The Book

The Storyteller is a series of extraordinary poetic journeys of hope and harmony, journeys that compellingly evoke spiritual re-awakening, compassion, and, indeed, heart-warming passion. Told with inspiring sensitivity, the destinations in "Spirit and Soul" encourage meaningful self-reflection and self-awareness, leading to the gripping destinations in "Whose World" in which the realities of war and oppression are deftly confronted and unmasked in a sophisticated yet easy-to-read storytelling style. Whatever your current personal situation, the final series of destinations will have you falling "In Love Again" ... all over again.

The Author

Author, Diplomat, and Social Commentator Thoko M. Banda graduated from The College of Wooster in Ohio where he studied political science. Recently retired from diplomacy, he dedicates his time to writing, public speaking, and consulting on socioeconomic cooperation. He lives in Germany with his wife and daughter.

Thoko M. Banda

The
Storyteller

Am amazing poetic journey of hope and harmony

June 2003 ©Thoko M. Banda

storyteller@manyika.de

http://www.manyika.de

Cover design and formatting by Herbert Voss,

voss@perce.de,

using pdfTEX, Version 3.14159-1.10a (Web2C 7.4.5)

Herstellung: Books on Demand GmbH

Printed in Germany, ISBN 3-8330-1055-X

With dedicated gratitude and love
To my parents, who taught me to live my faith
To my daughter, who motivates me to selfless purpose
To Ms. Forever, who inspires me to love
And
To the Almighty, whose grace and blessings abound

Contents

... Spirit and Soul

The river that is humble,
lies lowest and yet is
always the fullest

Aleke K. Banda

Happiness is when what
you think, what you say,
and what you do, are in
harmony

Mohandes K. Ghandi

SCARED

I am prepared...
Yet, quite tenderly
Scared

THE PAST...

The past...
Is like the sun
If we keep it behind us
But remain keenly aware
That it is there
It will watch our backs
Illuminate the way ahead
So we can see clearly
And progress on our way

Yet

If we stare
Into it for too long
It will blind our sight
Barely, but just enough
So when we now turn
To move on ahead
Blind spots prevail
We trip, we fail
We repeat the err
Again
To our past we stare

WISDOM

Where the stream
Of Common Sense
Ends
Begins
The river
Reservoir
Of Uncommon Wisdom
While Common Sense
Like Intellect
Is merely learnt
Uncommon Wisdom
Like no other
Is more profoundly yearned

If minds could feel
And hearts could think,
What a wiser world
We would live in

I CAN'T DECIDE

I can't decide
Which way to go
I really, really do not know

I want to serve
Give life, give birth
To hope, to faith, to livelihood
To those I love
And to those I should

I want to be happy
Truly
And to see
That those who live
Poorly
Inherit what's theirs
Justly
What's fair
To share

I cannot decide
Which way I should go
I really, really, do not know

CHILD

To be a child
To know to smile
For real
To know it all
While so small
To feel
The right to fight
To cry at night
Your meal
To be so picky
Nice when its sticky
For fun
Play in the rain
Through mud to run
And look
At picture books
Fantasy, tricks
Pretend
Time has no end
Even when
Its night
Turn out the light
God bless, sleep tight
Dear child

MOTHER

God had a seed
A special need
To entrust his heavenly treasure
He did find pleasure
Asked for her favour
To guard, to nurture
For earth's future
None other
Than Mother

THE CHAMP

In Nature's dictionary
Look up poetry
Defined simply
As Muhammad Ali

MEMORY

When I was young
I was small
I thought I knew it all
But my memory
It was empty
Now that I've lived
Now that I'm old
I do now know it all
But
Again I'm small
And as for my memory
Again, its empty

PRAYER

Pray
Everyday
Have your say

THE A-Z PRAYER

All
Blessed
Children
Deservedly
Enjoy
Feeling
God's
Healing
Impact.
Jesus
Knows
Love
Motivates
New
Ordained
Pleasures,
Quietly
Reflecting
Spiritual
Treasures,
Universal
Virtues,
Worthwhile
Xperiences,
Youthful
Zeal
Amen and amen

DEAR GOD

Hi God
My dear friend
Thank you for this day

Please help me make it a good story
For Your glory
Help me make you
Proud of me

I'm so glad this day gives me
The Opportunity
To put behind yesterday
Frustrations and shortcomings

You know what
Dear God
Today's a treasure
A present who's every moment
Is a unique pleasure

With fervent passion I will embrace
Tasks and experiences face
Inspire others
Appreciate Your wonder
Make dust in this our world

To do, to think, to feel
How little it does take
For happiness to be real
With You by my side
In my heart
My mind, my soul, my body
For myself to feel not sorry

I know how good it will be
To forgive
Those who seek to harm me
How fulfilling to tolerate
Those that try to frustrate

How special to make friends smile
To inspire the young
Give everyone
Gifts of love
Unconditional

How great to know
If due to me
One person does feel loved
And they'll go on
Love another one
And so on and so on

I know it won't be
Easy
Which means I won't be bored
That's why You have blessed me
For greatness yet unexplored

New romance
To make me dance
To not do or say
Things that may
Distract my way
May I not waste this chance

May compassion seeds be what I sow
So when to bed I go
Fulfilled I'll feel
Blessed still
Humbled, Your grace I'll know

MIRROR MIRROR

It's time
For me to show the world
What I am capable of
Excellence is now my master
I greet each moment, person and occasion
With the love I have abundant

Persistence
Until success is mine
I love being a miracle of nature
I seek like-minded companions
Surroundings, dreams, and goals
With the love I have abundant

I live
Each moment knowing
That it cannot be re-lived
My actions control my emotions
No matter what goes on
With the love I have abundant

When sad I'll laugh,
Confidence when I'm unsure
Conquer my fears, recall success
And focus on my goals
With the love I have abundant

I face the world
Humble and with humour
Every event that happens shall pass
Tools of tears and frustration repair my soul
With the love I have abundant

Heartfelt smiles and kind words
Are worth more than their weight in gold
Aim high, multiply my value a hundredfold
Announce my goals, take credit with humility
With the love I have abundant

My hopes, ideas and my dreams
I will never abort
I act in the present and plan ahead
For future presents too
With the love I have abundant

I will pray my thanks
I will pray for wisdom
But above and beyond all
I will be humble before the Great Almighty
With the love I have abundant

WHY ME? WHY ANYBODY

I catch myself
Try to understand
Hold my breath
No longer can pretend
Why me? I says
Why not someone else?

I say a prayer
God said he's my friend
I say not fair
There's gotta be an end
Help! I says
Put someone in my place

God answers clearly
Says come along with me
To those you love dearly
Here's your family tree
Help me! He says
Which one should take your place?

God is surprised
Taken aback
By my frowning eyes
Humour they do lack
Not they! I says
Please do look somewhere else

I know the jobless
Have run out of options
Soon maybe homeless
So I do support the notion
Not they! I says
Isn't there anybody else?

God asks about those people there
Those happy looking ones
Would you seriously prefer
That harm disrupts their lives?
Tell me! He says
Which one of them should be first?

God makes me an offer
After I realise
Its wrong to wish on another
To swap with them our lives
Have faith! He says
Your troubles will soon fade

My life is sure worth living
Priceless it is
Fear is merely False Evidence
Appearing Real
Why not me? I says
Why wish it on someone else

GIVE

When you have too little
Give
Learn to still live
When you have a lot
Help
So others too can get

When you are hurting
Love
So you can prevail
When you are loved
Inspire
Set another's heart on fire

When your mind is challenged
Soar
Let it fly above the mess
When your mind is calm
Embrace
Others' turmoil replace

When you are angry
Smile
'Till there's a twinkle in your eyes
When you are happy
Spread
Good cheer like flowers in bloom

When you are broke
Joke
A sense of humour invoke
When flush with cash
Reflect
The poor do not neglect

And when you feel strong
Uplift
The spirits of your friends
If I'm wrong
Forgive
Life will still go on

... Whose World?

I am convinced that life is
just a game, here on earth,
a game where no one
need be a loser

Og Mandino

The punishment of wise
men who refuse to
become involved in
government is to live
under the government of
unwise men

Plato

PALESTINE

My son
Your Son?
My brother
Our cousin
O' uncle
Young nephew
Dear neighbour
Why did you have to die?
Palestine
Hero
What hero?
He died to kill them
Who them?
Her son
Her son?
His brother
Their cousin
Her uncle
That nephew
O' neighbour
How many must die?
Palestine
Label, label, quickly label
Suicide bomber
Soldier, Martyr
That'll do
Lest we begin to feel
Let them die
Palestine.

AFRICA

We're tired of giving aid
Now they're dying
Of AIDS
We left them
Alone
Decades ago
To forge their own way
With our help
Of course
Any more crumbs?
Ok
Give them some grants
Forgive their debts
At the rate they kill each other
Brother against brother
For diamond and gold
They're young yet so old
Leaders like lead
Poisoning
Weigh the people down
They drown
In tears of despair
Hold them back
Going nowhere
Today
Like yesteryear
Where's the fresh air
For Africa?

REARRANGE

I want the world to know
I wish for you to feel
Make the abstract
Be more real
And for my people
Change
Rearrange
So, daily at least a meal
Their bodies
Stronger
Heal
Barefoot in the woods
Snakes, stones, thorns
Underfoot
Trying to survive
Heavy is the load
Water pail on her head
Her age?
She's barely eight
Stomach empty
Backbone supple
Young
Not yet ready
She's just a child
Yet look at her burden
Eyes red
Straining
Polluted

Fireside cooking
Lungs
Dusty
As the elites' Mercedes
Hurry past
In a whirl of dust
Oblivious
Contaminate her path
Oblivious
Toss discarded wrappers
Half-eaten cupcakes
Out speeding windows
Oblivious
Today she has not eaten
Tomorrow
Sorrow
Weak and without say
Work, no pay
All she can do is pray
Today
She's still a baby
How can she grow
If the world does not know
Her leaders do not care
Jet-set everywhere
Their lane is fast
Her needs are last
In tailored suits
They're in cahoots
Manipulate her roots

Start wars
Distort laws
In foreign lands
They hold out their hands
In her name
They play the game
Feel no shame
Who to blame?
The past
The colonial past
Those oppressive years
That raped the land
Robbed the wealth
That's who to blame
Feel no shame
Its not their fault
That the nation's vault
Has no bolt
At the back
Where none can see
The daylight robbery
The shirt off her back
Her right to be free
To eat, to play
To learn, to yearn
To run, for fun
Not away
Music, to hear
Not to fear

The leader
The cheater
She lives afraid
I want you to feel
What for her is real
Make it abstract
Change, Rearrange

PEACE

People
Everywhere
Are
Created
Equal

AMERICA

America
Disaster
Or master
From Asia, Europe and Africa
They travel so far

For centuries
Refugees
Get off their knees
Latino, Russian, Chinese
Their homelands they flee

Hope
For liberty's rope
They grope
Their boats barely float
From oppression they elope

Dreams
From scenes
Glossy magazines
Free schools, three jobs, build modern machines
Work hard to survive and try hard to fit in

Odd
In God
Trust bold
The people are told
No public prayer, young or old

Faith
Not safe
Replace
Gun culture they embrace
Neighbourhoods by race

Funny
Money
Running
Their life, their destiny
Survive if you have plenty

Multitude
Attitude
Foreigners misunderstood
The arrogance can be crude
Ancestral bonds forgot - how rude

The gloss
Its lost
A ghost
For some, even for most
From eastern shore to western coast

The Pres
No less
He does profess
World, you're in a mess
I'll put you in your place

The media
It feeds ya
Hysteria
A daily fear
Relentless propaganda

The people
Are gentle
They feel
Try to keep it real
Though trodden under heel

Healthcare
Nightmare
Can't bear
The burden's unfair
The frail need beware

Football
In fall
Baseball for all
Sunday's for the mall
The dollar stands tall

America
How great I are
Shortcut grammar
Superstar
World trendsetter

America...

BLOOD SPORT

Politics
Blood sport
Distort
The lies
Devious eyes
Behind the dark
Glasses
Misrepresent
Shut out irrelevant
Voters
Supporters
Naive reporters
Watch your back
And your pocket
Can't get them
In the docket
Immune
From the law
Trade
Your rights for more
What's left
For you to say
Except vote
But stay out of the way
Or become a clot
In their blood sport

GLOBALISATION

They are poor
And cannot read
Have big calluses on hands and feet
Sleep on the floor
Lack basic needs
For days their children do not eat

They break their backs
Through manual labour
Technology that's obsolete
What they lack
Leaders who're braver
So globally they can compete

Exploit their lands
Through corporate crimes
Without thinking of their rights
You rob them blind
For production lines
They have no chance to put up a fight

I see your greed
It makes me angry
I'll target those who're in the know
Patents indeed
Disgracefully
Rotten tomatoes at you I'll throw

When I trash your store
Disrupt your meetings
Although no jobs will I create
I'll even the score
Take police beatings
So that with them I will relate

I want to show
My deep frustration
And then return to where I live
I'll deal a blow
To globalisation
Having expressed what I believe

Now that I'm home
Had fun in Rome
I hope the world gets better
Oh, welcome
Mr. Postman
I'd better read this letter

Dear Globalisation
Campaigner
Thanks for your concern
Its in my nature
To not be bitter
But now they've closed the firm

My potatoes
And tomatoes
In my back yard they rot
The monthly pittance
The small remittance
Are gone, now I have nought

In your flat
I do hope that
You'll keep me on your mind
While you sip your
Cappuccino
My hunger drives me blind

I thought after
The factory closure
A better live begins
With resources
From the bourses
Of you and your campaigning friends

Who loses? Who wins?

RELIEF

Relief...
The victim hurts no more
Well, maybe he's still sore
At least
He's back at home

His eyes have softened
No longer frightened
He's probably in bed
Flowers, friends, Forgiven
Parental relief
Their son's still living

No doubt there is bravado
Embellishment even
It really doesn't matter 'cause
Their friend is sill living

Impatient driver off the hook
Relief for him as well
Hope that he is still in shock
Lesson learnt, forgiven

Thank God above
That through his love
The child is still living

NEEDLESSLY

A queen is crying today
Needlessly
A victim
Of the system
That continues to let him
Get away
Needlessly
With abuse
They refuse
To forbid and restrain him
From hitting
Needlessly
He is stronger
What can be wronger
Than to perpetually keep him
Free
Needlessly
Can't you see
The travesty
That's how they raised him
Mean
Needlessly
To mistreat women
And to keep them
Depending on him
Totally
Needlessly

Controls the money
Its not funny
She's owned not by him
At home
Needlessly
Her health
Family wealth
Belongs not to him
Alone
Needlessly
Its for the children
Next generation
Who're ignored by him
So long
Needlessly
Make her stop crying
Inside she's dying
Rehabilitate him
For life
Hopefully

IMAGINE...

Imagine...
How it must have been
Young girls were happy giggling
When the stranger man
With the gun
With his friend they started dragging
A muffled scream
A nightmare scene
The little girl was just thirteen
She disappeared
Parent's worst fear
No trace of where she'll go or has been
Interpol
Close the loopholes
That let them smuggle from state to state
Politicians
Diplomatic missions
You just talk the talk now its too late
Citizen
What are you thinking?
Stop supporting all the porn
To feed your habit
Is that it?
Do you really think that's why she was born?
Have you no mores?
They are not whores
They've been abducted, tortured - they fear
They are just girls
Thrust into your world
Please do not judge them by what they wear

All alone
They yearn for home
Their mother's arms they dream for most
What makes me sad
Is some decide
To treat them as forever lost
But if we care
Hear their prayer
It won't be long before they are free
If we do fight
Fight for their rights
They'll each be united with their family

SEPTEMBER ELEVEN

The tragic events in the USA
In September of zero one
Have left a gaping void
Just open air
In the Manhattan skyline

This empty space that we all see
Is profoundly surpassed
By a deeper void
Among young and old
For innocent lives that were sacrificed

For all the victims' families
Condolences and heartfelt prayer
We grieve with you
Condemn with you
These acts of senseless Terror

We share the pain that's centred
On DC and NYC
That radiates
We do relate
We are all one family

The vicious loss of innocence
Tragic loss of human life
Now weighs heavy
In our society
We resolutely unite

Against all those who do seek to
Undermine democracy
This cowardice
Just has no place
Has no humanity

The world agrees that justice must
Stamp out the terror's presence
And those who don't
Keep to God's laws
Will face our Maker's vengeance

The consoling acronym for Peace
In the shadow of this evil
Is that all
Of God's People
Everywhere Are Created Equal

We share your pain
And we do share your burning expectation
For justice and
That you will find
Grace, strength, divine protection

RESOLVE

Finally
A leader
Maybe two
Vilified by friend and foe
Motivated to go to war

Tragically
Round table
Insecurity council
Willing to appease the tyrants
Reeling towards irrelevance

Passionately
On capital streets
Demonstrators globally
Rally against the mighty
Pandering to entrenched dynasty

Compassionate
Defiant, irate
Simply cannot wait
Undermining the inspectors
Unilateral perspectives

Politicised
Public opinion
Bizzarely uniform
Most of the world against
The two, they buck the trend

Relieved
The deposed not grieved
A nation freed
Ungrateful to the liberator
Their distrusted perpetrator

Perceptions
For oil
War spoils
See conspiracy to re-map the region
Forget political executions

Patronized
By the autocratic
Leaderships undemocratic
Public sentiment manipulators
Newly vulnerable dictators

The victor
Benevolent superpower
Or global bullyer
Enforce laws of the bush
Legitimised by the blairbrush

Threatened
From city of romance
Pinochioid alliance
First Kyoto was flawed
Then criminal court declawed

Ultimately
Oppressed peoples braver
The world not any safer
Tyrants becoming history
Now governance and democracy

DEUTSCHLAND

I live in the land of Oliver Kahn
Of castles and bratwurst and the autobahn
In the land of many historical legends
Like Beethoven and Wagner and the Lutherans
Of Otto von Bismarck and Konrad Adenauer
And even the Towering Beckenbauer
Oops tut mir leid I forgot that old Franz
Evokes bitter memories for British soccer fans

When I tell the Deutsch people I come from Malawi
They say "Oh yes, I've been there. I've been to Hawaii"
The people are liberal in many a way
The language's confusing if this I may say
The women come smiling from rooms marked "Da Men"
The men they do hurry through doors signed "Her ren"

Beware on the freeways
They have no speed limit
Do not misinterpret
Their hearty "Gute Fahrt"

The Germans excel at what ever they do
Philosophy, literature, BMW
Respectful of nature, and opposing all war
Protecting your welfare, what you've worked hard for

City life is pleasant with bistros and parks
There's plenty to do even after dark
Be careful though when you put your foot down
The hounds have probably been out on the town

The cuisine is rich in its regional flavours
The beers are all legendry, their taste you will savour
The reason they tell you "auf wiedersehn"
Is because they do want you to visit again

MR. BIG MAN

Election
Democratically only once,
He won
Or was it through the barrel of a gun
Glued
Like bubblegum under your shoe
Stuck
He won't let go, he clings on
Hooked
Insists that he never cooked
The books
He can't understand why they don't
Add up
There's plenty here to go around
Plenty
He doesn't see the poverty
Dissent
The foreigners and dissidents
Invent
They don't accept that Mr. Big Man
Leader
Is loved so much by his subjects who
Expect
Their leader to build lush palaces
Galore
So they can live in luxury
Through him
Their Big Man who won't go quietly

Although
He does not know how to develop
Country
He's killing the weak economy
The food
Not enough for a family
The roads
All pot-holed, leading nowhere
Bridges
Just costly, wash away
The Jobs
Exist only in theory
The courts
Under the influence
Media
Muzzled, fed only morsels
The West
Richer but knows not to trust
The Big Man
Who pretends to empathize
With those
Who die needlessly
From Aids
Repression and poverty
Orphans
Whose only hope remains
To stop
Official corruption, rot
Covering
New Efforts to Pretend About
African

Development a smokescreen that's
Against
Democracy and liberty
Afraid
The people will vote for someone else
Who will
Hold them accountable for
The Wealth
Belonging to the ordinary
People
Who've suffered enough, can't you see
Educate
The children so that they can read
And write
To study beyond varsity
So that
Together they then rally
Get rid
Of the Big Man who has to go.

SEE

Please
Don't avert your eyes
Look them straight
In their lies
It's not a sanitizing campaign
Its war
No less, much more
They're out to kill
Children
Women too
Flowers and cheers they expect
From the widows and orphans they make
If you avert your eyes
Their lies
Become true
Victims lives
Campaign tools
Please
Don't avert your eyes

Please
Don't look the other way
They need you
To stay
They are not from a lower cast
They are not last
No less, so much more
Exploited then discarded

Families
Shamed histories
Forced into the shadows
Crowded out of the shade
If you look away
Social guises
Remain cruel
Their lives
Ghetto cesspools
Please
Don't look the other way

Please
Don't interrupt your gaze
They're getting bolder
Nowadays
We are not dispensable inventory
Human we are
No less, much more
Lay-off benefits - none
Working class
Pensioners too
The system takes for its coffers
From the banks , no credit offers
If you interrupt your gaze
Theirs are golden
Their parachutes
Our lives
They uproot
Please
Don't interrupt your gaze

Please
Don't neglect to see
Their cunning
Hypocrisy
Its not that there's no cure
The poor neglected
No less, much more
Left to persevere
Faceless
Young and elderly
Option is only to grin
Release body endorphin
If you neglect to see
Corruption
Distorts
Poor lives
Just pawns
Please
Don't neglect to see

Please
Don't squint out of sight
Lest you forget
To take the side
Of those who have no power
Its their last hour
No less, much more
Neutral is no option
If not for them
You're against

Lend to them your weight
Before it is too late
If you squint them out of sight
You side
With those of might
Frail lives
Further deprived
Please
Don't squint out of sight

... In Love Again

If I ever tell another
woman she's the most
beautiful I've ever seen,
it'll mean I live a lie,
because Beauty is you

There is no remedy for
love, but to love more

Henry David Thoreau

EMPTINESS IS ...

The feeling
When the woman I love says
"No, no more, not you, not me"

Hollow is...

The Heart
That's not allowed
To love you any more

Tough are...

The times
When your voice can be heard
By me, rarely

Hope
Love
Happiness
They're going, going, almost gone

ENDLESSLY

When will you decide
When will you see
How long must I wait
Endlessly

There's coming a day
Gotta be a way
For you and me to feel
Endlessly

Should I wait for you
Should I stay
Should I be sure
Do I still care
Endlessly

LOVE LOST

Where do I begin...

Oxygen, without you
Is difficult to breathe in
The sun above, without your love
Barely warms the skin

The way we've felt
And can feel again
Clearly can't be wrong
To love this way
To want, to care
Simply shows that we belong

Without a doubt
If it turns out
This love you wish to deny
I do confess
It is us we'll miss
And
Forever
Any other love that we profess
Will mean we live a lie

MS. FOREVER

I search for her
Ms Forever
I hurt for her
Ms Forever
Because she's never
Caught the fever
Of love
That I have
For her
Ms Forever

She's settling still
She deserves better
Than second best
Cruel fate, too late? No never
My soul knows where
To look for her
I search for
Ms Forever

SCARED OF LOVE

You're afraid to be wanted
Aren't you?
You don't want to be
Important
To someone else
To feel special
To be needed
Desired
You are scared to be loved
To know you're constantly
On another's mind
You probably don't even want to hear it
How pretty you are
Angel,
Star
Reluctant love

FAITH

Today
I got an answer to my prayer
Clearly
The good Lord did me hear
Always
When it seemed I could not bear
Days
That endlessly seemed to dare
Faithfully
With no doubts, no despair
Triumphantly
I have persevered

AGAIN

When she walks
She knows she belongs
And I fall in love
Again
The sun dims its radiance
Or so it seems
It winks
I think
As I fall in love
Again
The world, It spins
Its orbit confused
Gravity suspended
Time... blended
As I fall in love
With her
Again

HAPPINESS

I must confess
I feel happier
Than happiness
Thank you for coming back

CONFESSION

What I am trying to say
In my confused way
Is that since we met
I have but one regret

That I never learnt to compose or paint
So I could put to canvas, song, or dance
Your beauty and your radiance
Your grace and our romance

BEAUTY

If I ever tell another woman
She's the most beautiful
I've ever seen
It'll mean I live a lie
Because
Beauty is you
Its true
Love's pause is you as well
Fluttering butterflies
Wild flowers in bloom
Flamboyant setting sun
All bow before your delicate feet
In the dimming evening skies
Conceding that they do all pale
Deferring to the way
That you touch my day

BREATHLESS

A few short blessed breaths ago
An angel entered my life
Eyes, brown, they seem, or indigo
Smile drawing only love

Journeys begin always
With a single step
Lucky me, this one arrived
And made my heartbeat skip

Vision, passion, beauty, brains
Speechless I remain
This only partially explains
What I saw across the room

Judge me please not in haste
Accept me as I am, as me
I'll prove that I was worth the wait
Passionately

Your laugh, your dance, your voice, your walk
Womanly suppleness
Exposed navel nestled oh so close
Respectfully I brace

FALL

I hope you fall
No...
Not while walking
Blading, hiking, biking
Rock climbing
Or off your comfy bed
Cause then
You'd bruise your pretty face
Scrape your knees
Hurt, pain, embarrassed feel
I hope you fall
Hard, fast, once and for all
Realize
Of falling there's no need to fear
Cause falling
Never hurt a soul
Its only the sudden stop at the end
That can break
Strain, pain, really ache
But if you keep on falling still
Worst you can do is feel
Overflowing passion, love, bliss
Because of this
I hope you can overcome
And no longer miss
Your fear of...
Falling

FORBIDDEN

The hardest part was pretending
At the airport flight check-in
Ignoring each other
Like we had never met

We'd talked all night
In her room
Then mine
We'd come ever so close
To crossing the silky line

She'd spoke of her husband
I'd told of my wife
We'd welcomed the morning
Knowing each other's lives

The flight left on time
She sat rows ahead
It didn't take long
Before I heard her cheekily say
"Are you going my way?
May I sit? Is it ok?
I heard me whisper "Of course"
My inner voice warned "Don't let her too close"

As is often the case
The cabin air got chilly
She ordered a blanket
Now this may sound silly

I knew she would share
A mile high up there
But then, Should I dare?
Hmmm.. do I care?

Her husband is wealthy
Their marriage not healthy
My wife is aloof
Our union a spoof

Two couples each living
No love and no feelings
Divorce on horizon
Now intruding passion

Occasion inviting
Strangely exciting
First contact sublime
Her hand, not mine

Silence revealing
In that awkward pause
Urgency rising
What next? Who knows

Unruffled expressions
Deliberately so
Her breathing gets deeper
Oh...no...

A dangerous expression
That often precedes
The moment before
New lovers concede

My right hand guides her gently
She turns to her left
The space is not plenty
I caress her softness

Feathery tracing
Small circles and then
Anticipating
The exact moment when

She sighs her warm welcome
Inviting me in
Looking around us
We sheepishly grin

Back arched she knows
How deeply I'll touch
From my head to my toes
Its almost too much

On cue the plane captain
In misplaced monotone
Says "...we are landing
The lights are turned on"

Her radiance is blinding
There's a glow on her face
Our secret is binding
We withdraw our embrace

Her bright eyes alight
We begin to prepare
The cover was alright
No evidence there

The line we have crossed
Indelibly minted
Its meaning not lost
Its hope more than hinted

Up nearer the heavens
Our union complete
Now down to earth
Reality greets

She walks to her chauffer
Her husband is busy
My wife saunters over
Says "Why, you're back early"

The daily charade
Now will be replayed
Memories hidden
Love forbidden

CHANCE ROMANCE

You see me walk closer
To where you are
Sitting
Reclining
Basking
In the sun

I knowingly kneel
Right there by your side
I gasp, suddenly
"Oh no" I do say
"What is it?" you ask
Taken aback

I know I don't know you
We have never met
But I sadly have noticed
A spot of neglect
Right there I do see one
In the arch of your neck
A petal of passion
Asleep...
Now...
Awake

Oh no, there's another
Near sparkling brown eye
I feel you breathe deeper
I do hear your sigh
Eyes closed you welcome
As your hairline I trace
The caress of my kisses
What a beautiful face.

Pausing a moment
I ask you politely
"Your lips are inviting.
One kiss, will you let me?"
"Ah yes, only one,
But, please take your time"

Gently, most lightly
I begin to prepare
With your permission
To kiss you there
With barely a touch
I respect your space
You don't even watch
Your mind starts to race

As you begin to wonder
What happens next
My lips drawing nearer
You get the context
You let out a murmur
Or was it a purr
Your lips pout their welcome ...
... And then some

With butterfly softness
Our lips do embrace
Your welcoming warmth
Your womanhood I taste
As I struggle to speak
To say something smart
My tongue is a treat
As it works at its art

Deeply, completely
And then far less so
The motion repeating
You ask for much more
Warmed by soft thighs
My ears they are ringing
As you arch your back higher
My heart too is singing

Tears fill your eyes
As I come up for air
Unbelievable bliss
As I kissed you there
Sighing you savour
As gladly I see
A satisfied woman
Whose been loved totally.

OVERJOYED

Honey
You had me worried
When you said I should hurry
Are you alright?
Are you ok?
What could it be?
Please tell me

You urgently beckon me
You don't say a word
Your beauty's still dazzling
Years after we wed

The sun dress you're wearing
Accentuates
Every move you make
Sure resonates

Your backward glance catches me
Shaking my head
My eyes are absorbed
Where they have been led

I blush, I'm embarrassed
Thinking it shows
My instant acknowledgement
There in that clothes store

You turn around suddenly
Still without sound
What is the Mystery
Why does my heart pound

You ask me to help you
To make up your mind
Lingerie, black or blue
You need to find

In a voice spoken softly
So only I hear
You tell me you need it
Right now, to wear

"Don't move" you implore me
Hushing finger on my lips
I lose my control
As we touch at the hips

Without even giving it
Any more thought
Ignoring what happens
If we do get caught

You plead to me "Not yet"
But, oops, its too late
Pardon that I did not
Hesitate

How could it happen
In the shopping rush hour
In less than a moment
I welcomed your shower

You tell me you love me
I know that you do
What's also important is
I love you too

I see that not only
Your mind is so fertile
As you tease me and lead me
To the newly born isle

My joy overflows
When I hear the good news
The test you took shows
Soon we'll be more than two

DAZED

Thank you, most kindly
I appreciate your words
Its a pity your lover
Did not share your shower
I hope that the water
As it becomes warmer
Massaging your hair
Dripping off your ear
Cascading
Un-aided
To tickle
To nibble
Without realizing
There blood too is rushing
Yet being able
To locate your navel
Teasingly nibbling
The softness that's hiding
Your sensitiveness
Where a warmness
Flows out from the spot
That's now hotter than hot
The feeling complete
It tingles your feet
So all through the next night
Nerve endings alight
Your beddings caressing
Pleasures unending
Next day as you're working

You're still feeling perky
Right there where you are
Too tight feels your bra
The fabric you're wearing
Becomes too revealing
Warmness beginning
All over again

MAY I?

I won't say much
while I run my fingers lightly through your hair
I
just want to
take my time
letting you know
that I meant what I said
yes
snuggle
my dear
serenely
I'm whispering, I know
hope you can still hear me though
ah, you smile
I can hear
your heartbeat
settle
slowly
sleep
I'll be right here
whenever
you awake
my Ms. Forever
God bless....

...pause, be still, and hear
what the silence
conveys...